W9-CBS-793

SIX SLEEPY SHEEP

To our six little lambs
Jon, Todd, Jackee, Kevin, Brian, and Monica
We love ewe. — J.R.E. & S.G.T.

For Tess — J.O'B.

Text copyright © 1991 by Judith Ross Enderle and Stephanie Gordon Tessler
Illustrations copyright © 1991 by John O'Brien
Published by Caroline House
Boyds Mills Press, Inc.
A Highlights Company
910 Church Street
Honesdale, Pennsylvania 18431

Publisher Cataloging-in-Publication Data

Gordon, Jeffie Ross.
  Six sleepy sheep/by Jeffie Ross Gordon; illustrated by John O'Brien.
  24 p.: col. ill. ; cm.
Summary: This is the tale of six sheep trying various antics to fall asleep.
One by one each falls asleep. Rhythmic prose and playful illustrations
captivate young readers.
ISBN 1-878093-06-1
1. Sheep—Juvenile Literature. 2. Picture-books—Juvenile Literature. [1. Sheep. 2. Picture-books.]
I. O'Brien, John, ill. II. Title.
[E]   1991
LC Card Number 90-85728

First edition, 1991
Book designed by Katy Riegel

Distributed by St. Martin's Press

Printed in Hong Kong

10 9 8 7 6 5 4 3 2

SIX SLEEPY SHEEP

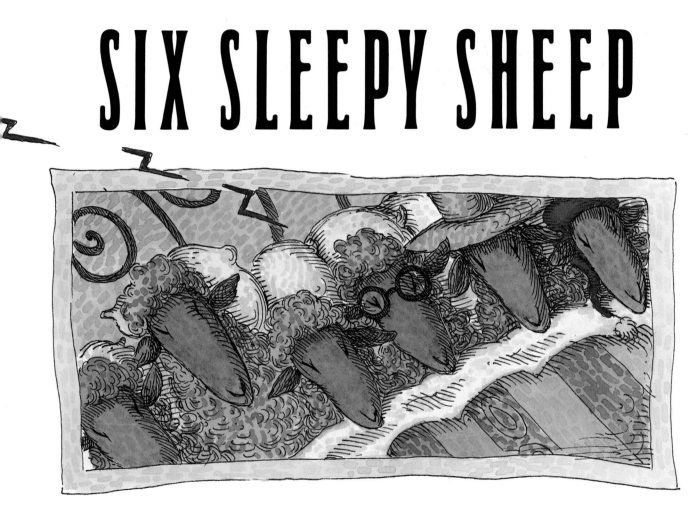

BY **JEFFIE ROSS GORDON**   ILLUSTRATED BY **JOHN O'BRIEN**

CAROLINE HOUSE

AAH! Six sleepy sheep slumbered on six soft pillows in one big bed

UNTIL...

one sheep snored.

"SHSHSH!" said five awake sheep.

And they gave that sheep a shake.

Now six sleepy sheep could not sleep.

SO...

they skipped in circles until they were swirly.

Soon one sheep snoozed.
Now five sleepy sheep could not sleep.

SO...

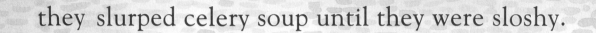

they slurped celery soup until they were sloshy.

Soon one sheep snoozed. Now four sleepy sheep
could not sleep.

SO...

they told spooky stories until they were shivery.

Soon one sheep snoozed. Now three sleepy sheep could not sleep.

SO...

they sang songs until they were silly.

Soon one sheep snoozed.

Now two sleepy sheep could not sleep.

SO...

they sipped simmered milk until they were snuggly.

Soon one sheep snoozed. Now only one sleepy sheep could not sleep.

SO...

he counted to seven hundred seventy-six.

Six sleepy sheep slumbered

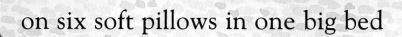

on six soft pillows in one big bed

UNTIL...